Kidnapper Island

Natalia Young

1st WORLD
PUBLISHING

Kidnapper Island

Natalia Young

© Natalia Young 2010

Published by 1stWorld Publishing
P.O. Box 2211, Fairfield, Iowa 52556
tel: 641-209-5000 • fax: 866-440-5234
web: www.1stworldpublishing.com

First Edition

LCCN: 2011920348
SoftCover ISBN: 978-1-4218-9197-2
HardCover ISBN: 978-1-4218-9198-9
eBook ISBN: 978-1-4218-9199-6

This material has been written and published solely for educational purposes. The author and the publisher shall have neither liability or responsibility to any person or entity with respect to any loss, damage or injury caused or alleged to be caused directly or indirectly by the information contained in this book.

The characters and events described in this text are intended to entertain and teach rather than present an exact factual history of real people or events.

Illustrations by Natalia Young

Translated from Russian to English
by Larissa Egner and Lilita Starokorova

This book is dedicated to the memory of my beloved daughter Olga Staver. She is a prototype of the main heroine in this story. Olga's honesty, bravery and responsibility towards those closest to her have been taken as the bases for Prisca's character.

CHAPTER 1

IN THE GREEN MONSTER'S CLAWS

*H*aving woken up with the first ray of summer sun, 10 years old Prisca turned off the alarm-clock. Her ears were still ringing with a few words from her dream: "Pick it up... find it... weave it..."

"Pick up... what?" the girl asked herself, trying to recall the whole dream vainly.

When she got fed up of doing so, she thought: "Silly thing! Just a foolish dream." Prisca hurried up to get washed and dressed. She braided two wide ribbons in her beautiful hair.

After that the girl entered her 5-year-old brother's room on her tip toes and shook his shoulder lightly: "Johnny, get up! We must hurry! Mum will be awake soon!"

Little Johnny, rubbing his sleepy eyes, thought of his Mum's birthday. Last night he and his sister had decided to gather a bunch of flowers from the nearest forest for their mum.

Prisca helped her brother to get dressed. They took two sandwiches and went out to the yard quietly.

The birds were just starting to sing. The summer day promised to be hot. The sky was full of freshness and clarity. A beautiful pink-yellow dawn blazed in the east. Prisca thought: "It's nice to go for a walk in the morning when it's not to school." The children were in a simply wonderful mood. Having their breakfast on the way and dreaming of Mummy being happy with their birthday present, the children reached the forest.

There were so many flowers in the woods, but the children had not noticed even one single blue flower.

"Mum likes blue flowers", said Johnny.

"But Mum says not to go far away from home," objected Prisca. And instantly she set their minds at rest, "we are not going too far, are we?"

And the children bravely went into the depths of the forest.

In one of the meadows they went through they saw a great number of outstanding beautiful flowers and they were all light-blue.

"Johnny," Prisca thought out aloud, "so that we don't lose each other, you recite all the rhymes that you know, and I'll listen to you, ok?"

"About Santa Claus as well?" asked Johnny.

"Any rhymes you know," Prisca made it clear.

With great pleasure Johnny began reciting the rhymes he'd learnt yesterday for his Mum. And the children joyfully went to gather the flowers, choosing only the most beautiful of them.

Step by step Prisca followed her brother's clear voice. Suddenly she noticed that it grew almost completely dark. The girl looked around.

The forest they were walking through now was not looking like the one they entered before. It was very weird and scary. The tree roots were half-bare. It looked like octopus tentacles were winding around them as if they were trying to break loose and walk away. The heaviest tree trunks stretched their dry squeaking boughs towards the scared children and clutched at the children's clothes. The sunlight hardly shone through the branches of those monsters joined together.

Frightened Prisca did not know where to go, trying to come out to the light. Without hesitation she tried to take her brother back home. It was very hard to walk, but they went on and on, never looking back but hoping to find the way home.

Suddenly, the children noticed the ground shaking under their feet.

"Where are we?" asked Prisca.

"I don't know..." answered Johnny sorrowfully.

Every step they took made the ground shake more and more. Prisca stopped and cuddled her little brother. She was so afraid to move any further...

Suddenly a loud rustling noise turned her attention to a huge cane bush. Some frogs were making their noise all around. A strange sizzling and something like a talking sound flew into Prisca's ears.

"It seems to be a swamp!" guessed Prisca.

She was right. It was a swamp, a very weird one.... There was one, and only one dry patch of ground in this swamp. The poor children stood on it, shaking with fear.

The thick green mud was moving slowly up and down around them. Sometimes it looked like a monster pulling his hands out of swamp, sometimes – like a gigantic frog was looking at the children... Suddenly the mud rolled itself up into plump lips. It let out a disgusting stink and weird sounds hard to understand. But clever Prisca managed to catch some of the words..." Two more frogs... it takes only... one touch..." Poor children's hearts were beating like mad! The children didn't know what to do...

Prisca pressed little Johnny to her breast and a few flowers dropped out of her hands. One flower fell down into the green mud, and the children could see that the little blue flower didn't sink into the swamp, but turned into a small and steady piece of land. It looked strong and Prisca took a risk to try it with her foot... It was a miracle! Prisca could stand on it!

"We can escape now!" whispered Prisca. "The flowers can help us!"

Unfortunately there weren't many of them in the bouquet and the swamp looked very big... Nevertheless Prisca threw down to the mud another flower, it turned into a knoll strait away.

"Johnny, I know you can jump better than your friends... You told me that... Please, do your best now! We must jump! I'll hold your hand, don't be afraid."

Prisca threw down a couple of flowers far ahead.

"Are you ready?"

"Yes..." said scared Johnny and they jumped.

Skipping from one knoll to another the children moved ahead across the swamp. The green mud went mad – it stretched its long dirty fingers towards the children trying to catch them...

"Well done, Johnny! I can see the land!"

"I can't any more..."

Prisca threw the last blue flower. At the same time the swamps slimy fingers caught Johnny's foot and pulled him down!

"Johnny!"

Prisca grabbed her little brother in her arms and jumped with him as far as she could!

"Hold oooon!'

It was a really big jump! They reached the land! They were safe now!

For the next two minutes Prisca couldn't even move a finger... She was exhausted! Having taken a deep breath Prisca finally calmed herself down but continued to lie quietly without any movement at all...

The swamp might have turned me into a frog!

She tried to imagine herself as a horrible green creature and made a wry face. Keeping her eyes closed Prisca put her left hand up and touched her hair.

"Ooh... It seems I'm alright... I am a girl," breathed out Prisca with great relief.

"Johnny! Where is he?"

Prisca jumped up from the ground and looked straight at her right hand which was supposed to squeeze her little brother's hand. But... it wasn't there! Her fingers had been holding a little green frog... She was horrified!

"No! No!" Prisca screamed. "My little brother! My Johnny!"

Tears began to flow down her face... She looked around calling his name again and again... But Johnny never answered. A frog can't speak.

"It's all my fault. The swamp has ruined you. What can I say to our parents now!"

Prisca cried bitterly, her face turned pale, she became weak in the knees and collapsed on the ground.

CHAPTER 2
NEW FRIENDS

A tiny voice made her come to senses.

"The Ocean water is flooding my house! Help!"

Prisca heard some rustle around her ear.

"Oh! It's not the Ocean, it's you!" said somebody. "Stop crying now! Don't you see my house is sinking in your tears! You will destroy all my stock. Stop it!"

The girl couldn't believe her ears, somebody was talking to her. Prisca wouldn't even think that in such weird place she could meet anybody except monsters... She dried her tears, open her eyes and saw little Mouse.

"That's better," said the little Mouse in calmer voice. "You can tell me now, what happened?"

The Mouse sat comfortably and got ready for the story. But Prisca still wasn't able to talk properly, so she just stretched her palm out, where tiny Frogy was sitting.

"It is my brother." was all Prisca could say without bursting into tears again.

The Mouse went deep in its thoughts.

"Tears are no help in sorrow," she said. "You don't know how lucky you are! No one has managed to escape from this swamp on their own two legs yet."

"But my little brother!" cried Prisca.

"Look how many of them are here," answered the Mouse pointing into the swamp with her small paw. "All of them had been just like you once."

Prisca looked around and noticed a lot of frogs crowding in the swamp. Big and small, hundreds of them were sitting and looking at her with regret and sadness. They were asking for help. The girl took pity on them. She put her head down. She didn't know how to help them...

"Shall we think together how we can help your brother?" said the Mouse.

"Yes! Yes! Please!" Prisca filled herself with hope to rescue Johnny.

Having had a little thought the Mouse continued:

"I think I know who can help you. There is small black house not very far away from here. The Black Witch lives in that house. Everybody calls her the Black Witch... She can release your brother from the swamps curse! But... I am not sure if she will like you... If not, I just could'nt begin to imagine what could happen to you!"

Prisca had no choice. She knew she just couldn't bring a frog instead of her brother back home. The swamp behind of Prisca wasn't so scary to her any more. Fear disappeared from her brave heart!

"I am ready to go to the Black Witch!" said Prisca firmly as if she was a grown up person.

"I'll do my best for poor Johnny," Prisca whispered to herself.

She was just about to set off but the Mouse kindly offered to let her have a rest near her little house. She said they should better go in the morning.

"I'll take you over there tomorrow," said the Mouse.

Prisca saw the sun was setting down beyond the forest. She was so tired and so hungry she decided to stay till the next day.

"My name is Pikky," the Mouse introduced herself.

"Prisca! Nice to meet you!" answered Prisca politely and smiled at her new friend for the very first time.

Pikky the Mouse brought some grains of wheat from her house. She gave them to Prisca and thoughtfully said:

"Please eat them!"

Prisca took the grains and ate them. She had never had anything better than that! Chewing carefully every single piece she really enjoyed the food and felt better. After such an unusual supper Pikky took Prisca to the brook deep into the forest. Clear and refreshing water brought Prisca her strength back. After drinking Prisca washed her face, took off one of her shoes and filled it up with water for Johnny. Another shoe was left near the brook.

Pikky and Prisca came back to Pikky's place. Prisca was very tired, she lay down on the soft lawn and dropped off to sleep immediately!

"Wake up! Wake up!" Prisca heard a little Pikky's voice in her sleep. Pikky was squeaking right into Prisca's ear and tickling her neck with a dry straw. Prisca woke up and remembered all her troubles straight away.

"Was it just a nightmare?" Prisca had a thought. She didn't want to wake up but she had to open her eyes to make sure that Johnny was fine... First thing she saw was her shoe and a tiny green froggy sleeping on it!

"No... It wasn't nightmare," whispered Prisca looking at Johnny with a great sorrow.

CHAPTER 3
THE KIND OLD CROW

A few strawberries and wheat grains were her breakfast. She drank clear water from the forest brook, it was her cup of tea that morning. Prisca put some fresh grass into her shoe. Then she made Johnny comfortable, tied the shoe up to her belt with her hair ribbon and followed Pikky the Mouse.

"We are going to see the Old Crow. He knows everything and everybody in the world! He can tell us the way to get to the Black Witch's place."

Prisca struggled to follow and keep up with the quick Pikky. The dry twigs of the wild bushes scratched her face and hands. Prisca's bare feet trod upon sharp rocks and thorns. She screamed faintly with pain but she kept following the Mouse trying to keep her eye on Pikky. The girl realised that the trees and bushes were not so scary as they were yesterday.

At last the travellers approached a big Oak tree. There was an old Crow sitting on a lower branch. His feathers had long lost their shine and his tail was bare. Wisdom was written in the Crow's eyes and one could guess that the Old Crow knew much!

Before Pikky opened her mouth the Crow kindly asked:

"What have you come for?"

The Mouse began telling him all the details about what had happened to Johnny.

"Would you please show this girl the way to go to the Black Witch?" finished the Mouse breathless from his rapid talking.

"You didn't have to talk so much. There is nothing more precious than time!" spoke the Old Crow wisely. And in the same moment as he was just about to fly off he said, "I'll help you, brave girl!"

Prisca thanked Pikky the Mouse for her help, kissed her good bye and rushed after the Old Crow. She turned around to wave to her rescuer one more time and Prisca saw that Pikky was upset and brushing away her tears. The Mouse felt sorry for this unfortunate, tired out girl!

The Old Crow was very wise. He understood that it was difficult for Prisca to follow him, that's why from time to time he sat on a branch and waited for her patiently. In her turn Prisca did her best running after the bird or walking as quickly as possible. After a while they reached a place where a few narrow and hardly visible paths divided. The Old Crow sat on a big rock which looked like it had been lying on the crossroad for a long-long time. The bottom of the rock sank deep into the ground. Tall grass and "death caps" were growing all around it.

The Old Crow pointed with his wing at one of the paths on the left and explained slowly:

"Follow this path, it will lead you directly to the Black Witch's house."

Then the Old Crow pointed at the top of the rock and warned Prisca:

"Please listen to me carefully. Can you see this the deepest crack in the rock? It will show you the way home, back into your village! You must remember it!"

"Thank you, my dear friend!" said Prisca and she was ready to continue her journey.

"Wait!" the Old Crow stopped her. He pulled a feather out of his tail, gave it to Prisca and said, "If you are in trouble, all you have to do is to hold this feather with your right hand and turn to the right on your right heel! And I'll help you! But remember: you can do it just once!"

Prisca fixed the feather into her hair, thanked the Old Crow one more time and and stepped onto the path leading to the Black Witch.

CHAPTER 4
AT BLACK WITCH'S

*I*t was much easier for Prisca to travel on her own. She could choose a smoother area on the ground to walk. She had to do it, because her feet were burning with wounds. Little Johnny the Frog slept in her shoe rocking at every Prisca's step.

"I don't understand why the Black Witch might not like me." Prisca was thinking loudly. "My parents love me, my friends love me, why shouldn't she? I've got lots of friends. I am not a bad girl."

Prisca suddenly stopped and turned around as if someone could hear her praising herself. She didn't see anyone, but her cheeks still blushed with shame though.

"It's good that no one could hear me," she calmed herself. "But I am not so good... All these troubles wouldn't have happened if I had listened to the adults and hadn't taken Johnny to the woods."

The Sun had generously shared its warmth with everyone around. Only the greenery under the trees trying to keep their roots moist had been hidden from the Sun.

Prisca was very tired and thirsty but she didn't stop. Finally on a piece of flat land she noticed a wall made of bricks. The tall dark grey tiled roof had been built above the wall. When she got closer Prisca saw built-in metal doors. She couldn't find either a key-hole or a handle in the doors. Prisca tried to open them but the doors didn't budge... When she knocked on the doors with her finger she couldn't hear a sound! Prisca drummed onto the thick metal with all her little fist's strength. No reply. Having hurt her hands Prisca realised that it will be really hard to get to the Black Witch. Upset Prisca leaned against the wall...

"Why can't I fly?" Prisca raised her head up to the sky and remembered the kind Old Crow.

There was the flat wall above her head. It was so high, no one could climb on it.

Prisca was suffering from hunger, thirst and tiredness, so she sat under the wall till the evening. When the sun set Prisca saw that her little frog Johnny jumped out of her shoe and set on a small rock, which the girl hasn't noticed earlier. At that moment Prisca had a brain wave! She forced herself to stand up. Then she took that little rock and hit it to the wall with all her strengths. The loud sound came out and made her jump!

A moment later Prisca heard a husky man-like voice:

"Who is disturbing my peace?"

Then the locking bar clanked and the squeaking doors creaked open. Prisca saw a tall round-shouldered old woman. She had an earthy-yellow face, a sticking out chin and the tip of her nose could reach her lips. The Witch was so skinny that her long black gown hung loosely on her as if she was a hanger. She wore a tall black hat with small cocks. Her long, grey, untidy hair sticking out from under her hat had never been combed.

Prisca was even frightened a bit by such an ugly appearance of the old woman. But she did her best to try not to show her fear.

"Good day, ma-am! My name is Prisca. Sorry for disturbing you but I really need your help, please!" said Prisca. She had prepared these words beforehand.

Then Prisca showed Johnny the Frog to old woman and told her what happened to her little brother.

"Hmmm... How much will you pay me for the help?" asked the Witch.

Prisca kept her head, she remembered about a silver ring with a crystal stone. It was a present from her mum. Prisca had never parted with this ring before. The very first time Prisca took the ring off and held it out. The Witch took it, turned it round in her bony hands and replied rudely at last:

"Not enough!"

"But I haven't got anything else." confirmed Prisca.

An angry look flashed from under old woman's hat. She fixed her eyes on Prisca's beautiful golden hair.

"If you haven't got anything else, give me your hair!" mumbled the Witch with her toothless mouth.

Prisca looked at her long, tight plait sadly... She'd hate to lose her beautiful hair.

Nothing to worry about, it'll grow soon, she thought and nodded her agreement.

Secretly Prisca pulled out of her hair Crow's feather and closed her hand over it. The Black Witch took huge rusty scissors out of her big pocket. Pleased with herself she cut Prisca's hair pitilessly. Then the Witch pulled a red ribbon out of the hair with disgust and threw it on the ground. The girl picked it up and carefully tied it up to the belt, above her skirt.

I might need it, she thought. She couldn't think what to expect from the old witch.

"Still not enough!" croaked satisfied Black Witch, feasting her eyes upon cut hair in her hands. "I have got some jobs for you. You'll serve me for some time and then I might do what you ask me to."

"Yes, ma-am!" Prisca replied as soft as possible trying to melt the old woman's heart. The Black Witch dug her skinny fingers into the girl's shoulder and dragged her to the yard.

"I'll show you what to do," she said and bolted the door. Then the Witch locked up a padlock and put the key into the same pocket where she had her scissors.

Entering the witch's place Prisca realised that it will be much harder to get out of there than going in.

There was a brick wall all the way around the huge property. Dark and thick woods spread wide over the wall. The witch's house was made of the same grey bricks as her wall. There was a big metal tank near the porch.

Prisca's heart jumped with joy! She noticed a pond, it wasn't very far from the house. Now she worried where to put her little Johnny the Frog!

"Every morning you have to clean the yard and fill up the tank with fresh water from the pond," the Witch pointed to the tank. "After washing dishes and tidying up the house you'll weed my vegetables."

The old woman took Prisca into the house. It was dark and not a cosy place. The small iron-barred windows didn't let any daylight come through. There was a thick grey spider's web all over the house. The first room Prisca went into looked like a kitchen. There were different kinds of dirty smoked dishes on the shelves nailed to the walls. A big table was full of pottery and glass jars of all shapes and sizes. In the second room Prisca could only see some massive old chests screwed to the floor. All of them had been locked with big padlocks.

The third, furthest room was almost empty. There was only one thing a wide oak bed covered with dark and rough matting in the left corner of the room. A black curtain screened witch's bed.

"Don't even think to touch this door!" said the Black Witch strictly, pointing at the door with her finger. The girl saw an iron-clad door deep in the wall opposite the bed. Three steep steps led you down to the door...

The Witch painfully seized Prisca by her shoulder and took her out of the house. She guided the girl to the wooden shed, which was behind the house. The old woman threw an armful of straw under the shed wall.

"You will sleep here! There is no space for you in the house," she said coldly. After that she went home and brought a bowl of porridge, some vegetables and herb tea.

"This is your dinner," she said. "Early in the morning when the birds first sing you will begin your work!" The Witch moved out of the house and locked the door behind her.

Some very hard days were to come to Prisca. Very early every morning, when she was cleaning the yard The Witch went to the forest. She never used the front door to go out. Prisca couldn't understand how The Witch passes through the wall made of bricks? The Black Witch just kept disappearing...

I wonder why she goes to the forest every morning, Prisca thought to herself. Maybe just for a walk...

Within two hours the old woman usually appeared back in the yard. Then she would go to the garden, pick up greenery and herbs go home and disappear behind the mysterious iron door... By that time Prisca had to tidy up indoors. During the rest of the day the house was shut off to Prisca!

After tidying the house the girl had to fill up the tank with water. This was the hardest work for Prisca. The bucket was so big; its bottom scraped the ground when she was carrying it. Although Prisca filled up only half of the bucket she had to keep stopping to rest. After the tank was full of water she went to the garden and weeded the vegetables. She worked there till the sunset. The garden was so huge. Prisca worked hard but she couldn't finish all weeds over the whole garden during the day. The Witch was always very angry with her.

Having finished her job Prisca run straight to the pond where Johnny had been waiting for her. It was the best and long-awaited time of the day for her! She sat by the side of Johnny the Frog and spoke to him till late night... The Frog wouldn't answer but she knew that Johnny understood everything. Talking to him Prisca remembered their friends, family and all the funny things that ever happened to her and Johnny. In time Prisca met new friends caled lightning bugs. They were flying around her head like a white cloud lighting up everything in the night darkness. They understood Prisca's talking as much as Johnny did.

The days passed by. Every evening the Witch said to Prisca the same thing:

"You have only worked off your lunch today!"

CHAPTER 5
THE ESCAPE

One night Prisca fell asleep on her straw bed after a very hard day. Suddenly she jumped up at midnight... Her heart was beating fast! She heard a well-known voice in her dream again:

"You picked it up... good! Now try to find..."

"What did I pick up?" Prisca was thinking hard. "Maybe a bunch of flowers? Yes! Blue Flowers! That's it! The flowers helped us to cross the witch's swamp!"

This time she took her dream more seriously than she did the first time at home.

What do I have to find? She asked herself again and again...

Morning birds singing interrupted her thoughts. The old woman was already coming to wake her up.

The new day seemed to Prisca to go quicker. Trying to find the answer the girl didn't even feel any tiredness. After sunset, when the Witch as usual had gone home, Prisca went to the pond. Having sat on the soft grass she told Johnny about the mysterious voice in her dream.

"I have to find something. But what exactly?" asked the girl and looked at her brother as if the green frog could answer her.

Suddenly she heard a loud noise. Fresh soil fell on her shoe and a cute little snout came out of the ground.

"A mole!" she shouted happily with a surprise and clapped her hands.

"Sorry for my curiosity," apologized the Mole lisping in its funny way. He was struggling out of the hole. "I have listened to your night talks for a long time... Generally speaking I am very curious! I understand you are in big trouble... And I have to tell you that this old woman will never keep her promises! I am blind but anyone can envy me and my good ear."

As the Mole got out of his hole he continued his quick funny talking:

"Ah... Sorry again! I didn't introduce myself. My name is Moly! I've heard your names already nice to meet you! I am ready to be your friend!"

Prisca hadn't been surprised that underground creatures in this forest could talk. She looked at her new friend with delight. The Mole didn't even let her open her mouth.

He pointed at the Witch's house with his paw and continued:

"The evil swamp is hers! She made it years ago... Not only this one but many other green traps. They are all around! Everywhere! Swamp folks can't cross it... If they try they sink as a rule. Apparently we can go in that direction where people are coming from. A Green Monster turns people into frogs and never lets them go! Your brother is very lucky... You took him out! I can't understand only one thing why the Witch needs so many frogs? What does she do with them? I don't know."

"What we do now?" asked Prisca.

"Run! As soon as possible! Just run!" said Moly firmly.

"What about Johnny? I can't go home with a frog," replied the girl and put her head down. Moly rubbed the back of his head.

"Hmmm…" he went deep into thought. "You have to find a way to turn a Frog back into the Boy!"

Prisca's heart missed a beat. Moly's words were the answer to the question she was struggling with…

"But how can I find it?" she asked.

"My wormhole is near the Witch's basement. I've built my house over there on purpose. As I've said I am very curious… I can hear everything the Witch does in her house! At night time she makes some magic drinks and even some poison! She comments about everything she does. And I have even seen all the labels she marks the pots with! But the drink which could bring you back to norma." Moly stopped for the moment. "I haven't heard her make it for ages."

Prisca lowered her head in sadness. She didn't know what to do next!

"Don't give up, kind girl! We will hope for the best! I'll keep listening to the Witch every night. One day I'll get news for you and come to see you! Cheer up!"

Moly waved goodbye to Prisca and went underground.

"Thank you!" said Prisca before Moly was gone.

She lay down on the grass and rolled comfortably into a ball near Johnny the Frog. She was thinking of Moly. In spite of being so small he sincerely wanted to help her! Prisca had no doubt about it! For the very first time since Prisca arrived in this scary place she felt calm and good. As if somebody took half of her troubles away from her… The ground heated by the sun during the day warmed her up. Soft, fluffy greens wrapped Prisca gently and carried her into a deep sleep…

Only several days passed but it was like ages for Prisca. From the time she had met her new friend she stayed near the pond all night long. Waiting for Moly Prisca listened for every little noise. But usually deep in the night she became overcome with tiredness and sleep.

One night Prisca was sitting near the pond hardly believing she would hear from Moly again. Then suddenly she heard a little voice from underground. Moly was calling her name and he sounded very excited!

"Prisca! I've heard something! I've heard! And I remember every single word!"

Moly's fluffy figure appeared from underground.

"I heard clearly that the Witch rubbed her hands coming into the basement, and then she touched her pots and glasses and said: "What have we got here today?"

Moly copied the old woman's scary voice as good as if he was an actor.

"Have I run out of anything? Yes... I have. I've run out of the drink which brings you back to normal." continued Moly. "I'll need a lot of it very soon!" This is what she said! Then I've heard a dreadful noise, the Witch laughed and whispered: "This silly girl will never get the magic drink! Johnny the Frog will be a frog forever! Yes!"

Moly took a deep breath:

"The Witch poured a prepared potion into small glass jars. She marked those jars with triangles! She said it."

Prisca was so happy to hear that! She bent towards Moly, brought his snout nearer to her face and kissed his cold nose with a loud smacking kiss!

Moly's pleased snout stretched out in a big smile! He was glad to make this kind girl happy at least for a short moment.

"Can you please bring me that magic drink?" asked Prisca.

"Of course, I can, but..." hesitated Mole. "I can't see anything. How will I find the triangle mark on the jar?"

A fresh solution came to him quickly. He turned around and said loudly:

"I've got friends! I'll talk things over with them!"

The next moment he disappeared under the ground...

He came back very soon and brought his friends with him. One after another they appeared from under the ground. Prisca counted nine moles. All of them looked very much alike. But Prisca did recognize Moly straight away! He was the quickest one. Nine moles stood in line in front of the girl.

They are all my friends! said Moly and called out their names. The last one was called Trocky. He was the biggest mole and looked very important!

"Having friends in the market is better than having money in the chest!" he said slowly. "So... here we are: 18 of us out of the hundred came to help you, brave girl. And I have already got a plan!"

Trocky pointed at the hole where they all came from and continued:

"Tonight we begin to dig this underground tunnel bigger. The other 9 moles will dig a tunnel under the wall for you, my brave girl! Then we will connect it with witch's basement. I think it will take us 3 nights to finish this work. When it is ready, you and your little brother can go to witch's secret room through her basement! You will find the magic drink and rescue your brother!"

Trocky spoke slowly and clearly. Then he found a small dry stick and drew the plan of the underground walk on the sand.

"But it is dark out there! She wouldn't see a mark on the jar" said clever Moly. No one even thought about it...

"Maybe lightning bugs could help me?" replied Prisca. She was always followed by a cloud of lightning bugs. It was just above her head. The bugs began to move merrily in front of her face after these words.

"Look! They are ready to help!" Prisca smiled with gratitude. She was happy!

Not wasting precious time, the moles rushed to the work. They dug the ground, with no rest, no asking questions. The dug out soil was stored at the tunnel entrance, Moly and Trocky moved it to the pond. After one hour's work Prisca brought some fresh vegetables from the Witch's garden to feed the diggers. She was taking a risk because the Witch could notice they were missing... Moly called up all the hardworking moles. All together the 18 friends sat down in a circle for a little rest and a meal. Eating up the rich and juicy carrots Moly said:

"After you, Prisca, leave this place, there will not be one carrot left in this garden!"

"We shall take care of it!" added pleased Trocky.

All 18 moles burst out laughing until they cried! Prisca couldn't help laughing too...

Prisca moved back under the shed to sleep in the night. The girl wanted the Witch to get into the habit of waking her up at the same place...

But something strange seemed to have been happening to the Witch the last two days. She kept disappearing somewhere in the early morning as usual, but for a much longer time... Luckily she didn't notice the loss of vegetables. The Witch looked very anxious. She was picking up greens and herbs from her garden automatically, having paid no attention to things around. Sometimes she whispered or pronounced loudly some numbers...

One night Prisca met her little friends again. Trocky was happy to report to her:

"Everything will be ready in three hours!"

"You must run tomorrow morning when the Witch leaves for the forest!" added Moly.

Suddenly somebody appeared from the underground tunnel. It was Proly, the mole. Stammering with excitement he said:

"I wo-wo-worked near the basement, I h-h-heard that the Witch is going to do something bad to you, Prisca... She wants to make you to forget your home, your parents, your brothers everything and everybody! She has already prepared a drink which will take your memory away!"

Having said that Proly covered his face and mouth with his paws. Smart and quick Moly without saying anything went into the hole. He came back straight away carrying a mug in his paws. This mug looked very similar to one in which the old woman usually brings morning tea to Prisca.

"Does it look like the usual one?" Moly asked.

"As alike as peas!" answered Prisca. The girl guessed what to do next! She filled up the cup with the water from the pond. Put it under the shed and covered it with straw.

The tunnel building was coming to an end. Prisca had done up her hair in a tight plait with a long green stem instead of ribbons. She hid the crow's feather in it. All this time she had kept it safe under the straw. Prisca fell asleep in the morning.

The old woman woke her up in a very unusual sweet way she stood in front of the girl and smiled... There was a basket full of something and covered with old clothes in her hand. The Witch was holding a mug in her other hand. When Prisca sat down on the shed floor, the old woman gave her the mug saying:

"Ok, drink it, girl! it's good for you. It will give you strength!"

Prisca was confused a bit...

"Thanks, ma-am!" she said and took the mug. The Witch was staring at her! Prisca really didn't know what to do...

Suddenly Prisca remembered a funny game her father used to play with her. He would take her attention away from him, make her look somewhere else, and then gently tweak her nose.

Prisca stretched out her hand instantly and said:

"What is that? Something huge...!"

As soon as the Witch looked away the girl swapped the mug for the one hidden before! And then she drank all the clean water from it. The Witch made sure that Prisca had drank it all then commanded with a rough voice:

"Back to work! Now!"

The Witch went to the forest, on her way she was muttering to herself:

"He can't wait! It's no rush at all... There is still time, my dear!"

Prisca heard it and thought:

"What is she talking about? There wasn't anyone there! It was just joke..."

As soon as the Witch disappeared, Prisca ran off to the pond. She tied up her shoe with a ribbon around her waist as she had done before. Prisca put Johnny the Frog inside her shoe and came to the underground tunnel. The moles had covered it with dry and fresh sticks just in case. Prisca removed sticks from the entrance. She was so scared to go into the dark place! Prisca had to kneel to get into the tunnel. Thanks to the Lightning Bugs they didn't let her down. They'd been waiting for her under the ground. It was very damp and cold down there. Prisca felt sorry for her little friends the moles...

"Poor moles... How can they live in such a horrible place!"

Very soon she felt hot because of her movement. She worked hard. The tunnel seemed to be endless. At the junction she turned to the right, as it was in the plan. Finely she was so tired, she just wanted to lie down and rest. But Prisca knew that the Witch would come back from the forest soon. So the girl kept moving!

"At last!" she heard Moly's worried voice. Moly and Trocky had been waiting for her, ready to finish this life saving job! They dug the ground and opened a hole into the Witch's basement. Prisca could smell a mix of mould, burnt hair and herbs from the room. As a shining cloud the lightning bugs came into the basement. It was very dark but Prisca could see many shelves, one above another. There were lots of big and small pots and glass jars over there. Prisca rushed to the shelves to look through the pots. She was in a hurry but she moved carefully because she didn't want to break anything. The time passed quickly but Prisca couldn't find the pot marked with a triangle. She was in a panic! Prisca new that in a few minutes the old woman would be home! It seemed absolutely impossible to find the pot...

The Witch might have used it for somebody else! thought Prisca. She remembered that the old woman was carrying a basket full of something this morning... Prisca burst into bitter tears!

Suddenly all the lightning bugs fluttered to the bottom shelf. Prisca guessed that her little friends were trying to tell her something! She threw herself down to them. The lightning bugs surrounded a little pot marked with triangle! They found it! The pot was hidden behind of a few huge jars! Prisca carefully put them down on the floor and reached for the little pot. Finally she got it!

Just at that moment Prisca heard the old woman unlocking the front door and telling her off!

"Where are you? bad girl! Your work isn't done! You haven't run away, my dear, have you? If you have, don't worry, I'll get you! And I'll teach you a lesson!"

Prisca slipped into the underground tunnel together with her little friends. She was scared and she didn't feel at all tired! They moved away quickly! Moving back with the pot in her hands was very difficult... Prisca rubbed her sore knees, they were really painful! But the brave girl carried on crawling quite fast. In a few minutes Prisca heard Moly's voice. He was somewhere behind her:

"Prisca! Look! I found it in the Witch's basement... It's yours!"

Moly put something in her shoe whilst running, but Prisca had no time to look what it was!

In a while Prisca saw the light. It was the way out! Prisca hardly got herself out of the tunnel. Then she rushed along the path away from The Witch's house, and it took some time before her eyes got used to the light again... Prisca turned around and saw a black gown behind her! The Witch was chasing her! The old woman moved her long legs so fast! She screamed:

"Stop! Stop, nasty girl! Give me back my magic drink! I'll get you!"

Prisca held the pot very tight in her hands and she was running so fast! Prisca hoped that the old Witch would soon be exhausted, but she didn't think she would be. The distance between her and the old woman was shortening so quickly... Very soon Prisca's feet gave way under her, she couldn't feel them. The Old Witch was so close! Prisca lost her breath... the Witch's long bony hand had been stretched out ready to catch Prisca! Prisca pulled the crow's feather out of her hair, stopped suddenly and turned around on her right heel to the right! She stopped dead in her tracks as if she was frozen with eyes closed tight... She thought The Witch would grab her in a second...

When Prisca made herself open her eyes she saw something really amazing... The old Witch was standing still very close to her with arms stretched out. But it seemed she couldn't move a finger! Prisca took deep breath, came closer and touched the Witch. She was as hard as wood and she was icy cold!

Prisca dropped into the grass with a great relief. When her breath came back to normal she took her Johnny the frog out of her shoe. All of the sudden she saw her little ring in the bottom of shoe!

That's what Moly put in my shoe! she thought. My dear little friend...

Prisca's eyes moistened, she felt sorry she couldn't say "Good bye!" to all friends who helped her...

"Thank you, friends! I will never forget you!" she said.

Prisca was still holding the pot tight. She opened it and poured some drink into Frog's mouth. In a few moments a thick fog came from nowhere... It was sparkling brightly. Prisca couldn't bear it and she had to cover her eyes with her hands! Next moment she heard:

"Prisca!"

Johnny the Boy jumped out of the magic fog and threw himself on Prisca's neck! Johnny was back! Prisca gave him a big hug and kiss, she couldn't believe her eyes! She was crying with happiness!

CHAPTER 6
MEETING BUGY-BAGA

They were not going to waste any time, Prisca took her brother to the fork in the road. On their way the children were sharing what they had gone through...

"I thought earlier that a miracle could happen only in fairy stories," Prisca said.

"The Witch was so scary... But now she is much better!" replied Johnny.

"You are right! She looks much better now!"

Children burst out laughing in the woods silence...

In forty minutes the children reached the place where a big rock should be at the fork in the road as they thought. But they saw a hole in the ground and fresh soil at the place where the rock has been not long before! Nobody could move such a huge rock, even the strongest man in the world couldn't... Prisca didn't understand what had happened! The rock had disappeared! The children were confused...

"Who did it?" Prisca thought. "Where do we go now?"

Prisca tried to concentrate and remember in detail the rock's cracks. Which path those cracks were pointing to? But she was unsuccessful... Johnny tried to help his sister. He stretched out his hands holding them in fists and said:

"There are two sticks in my hands, one long one and one short one. You choose! If it is long stick we go to the right path, if short to the left," he said being very proud of himself!

Prisca slapped brother's little fist. There was a short stick in it. Well, they went to the left!

The forest wasn't very thick but the trees there seemed taller than usual. Very soon the children came across a meadow covered with wild strawberries. They squatted down and refreshed themselves with the juicy and ripe berries. They really enjoyed them! After they'd eaten Prisca looked at her brother and said:

"Now you look like a big strawberry!"

Johnny's face, hands and shirt were red because of berries. The children laughed.

"When we get home, grandma will bake cherry doughnuts," said Johnny. "And it'll be a big cherry!"

The children had a little rest and went on their way. Very soon they got to a big woody hill. Now they had to move up the hill and it was difficult!

"We must see a village when we are on the top! Then the people could help us to get home ! "

The children had to rest a lot because of the hard climb. Sooner or later they heard a noise coming from the very top of the hill.

"We'll be home soon!" rejoiced Johnny.

The noise became louder and louder. In a while the children stopped near the edge. Prisca had learnt to be careful. She pushed Johnny's head down to the ground gently, she wanted him to lie down.

She sat behind a big bush to hide herself. Then Prisca parted the branches and saw something amazing: there was a deep cut just at the very top of the hill! This hole was so big, no one could see its beginning nor its end. The edges of the wall around the hole were made of rock. Prisca noticed wooden houses covered with straw down at the bottom, and there was a huge palace in the middle of the hole. It was really big, its roof was above all the other buildings there. The palace was very special and very beautiful! The windows frames were decorated with precious stones shining on the sunlight. Wide steps with golden handrails led to a tall door. There were luxury flowerbeds and lawns all around that beautiful building.

To the right Prisca saw many people doing backbreaking work. Five of them were pulling a big cart full of huge rocks. Bending their backs they moved towards the wall with all their might. Another five men were pushing the cart at the back. There were many carts like that following one after another. Strange, ugly and very tall creatures were standing all along the carts way. They were holding some whips and bludgeons. Creatures had pear-like-heads, camel's ears and big black eyes. Their skin was covered with green scales which looked like fish scales. These monsters were hitting the workers mercilessly. The poor people couldn't stand it, they were falling down on their knees... moaning and screaming they were heard everywhere!

A crack of the metal made Prisca to look to the right. She saw a big metal shield, it was the door. With a noisy crack it was coming up along the iron railing and opening a high ladder. After a while some people appeared on it. They were coming down the stairs in dense line with their heads dropped low. Prisca could hear a sad chain noise, she could see shackles on their feet. These slaves were escorted by green creatures as well...

"If I only could help these suffering miserable things!" thought Prisca sadly. She couldn't take her eyes from them and she didn't notice someone was pulling her skirt. She heard "Sh-h-h!" and turned around. A dark-haired lad around of 18 years old was holding his finger across his lips; he wanted Prisca to keep silence.

"What are such small children doing here?" he whispered. Without waiting for an answer he nodded his head to the side and ordered:

"Follow me quickly and quietly!"

The children obeyed. They bent their backs and followed him trying not to make any noise.

Coming down the hill was just as difficult as going up. From time to time the children had to slide down grabbing onto a tree's branches or a nearby plant. The young lad helped Johnny to come down and held Prisca's hand.

The lad's name was Tom. He managed to escape from this terrible place when he was working on the very top of the new building wall...

It took quite a long time to get down from the hill. When the three escapers came down, it was already dark... They made haste, they wanted to go away from this scary place.

"Who lives in that palace?" Prisca asked.

"The owner of everything you saw in there, Prisca, is the cruel, one-eyed giant monster called Bugy-Baga," answered Tom.

"Who are those creatures with whips and sticks?" carried on questioning curious Prisca.

"They are Goklags. They are The Monster's slaves and they are ready to die for him!"

"Who are those poor people then?" Prisca couldn't stop.

"If you are here you must know the Black Witch?"

"Sure! Of course! But she is the Wooden Witch now!" Johnny said merrily.

"Unfortunatelly she stays like that only until it rains... This Witch catches people in her ponds and turns them into frogs," answered Tom.

"I was a frog too..." Johnny jumped up as if he was proud of it.

"You were very lucky to escape. Your sister is definitely a smart, brave and quick girl," Tom said to Johnny. "All other frogs will stay like that till the Bugy-Baga wants them as slaves in his new buildings. Then The Witch turns them into people and sells them to Bugy-Baga for treasure stones... Straight on the ponds banks the Goklags put the people into irons and took them into Bugy-Baga's underground." Tom finished his sad story.

"It's embarrassing to say but I was a green frog too..." added Tom looking to Johnny with a sad smile.

"I have never-ever seen any houses built inside the top of the hill... So strange!" said Prisca.

"Hmmm... The Monster is very sly and clever. He wants to control his enemies from the top of the hill and he has hidden himself in a hole..."

It was completely dark when the tired travellers decided to stop under the fluffy bush on the little hill. They hid themselves between branches and sat there comfortably. Tom got out of his pocket a piece of rice bread and divided it into three. He gave two pieces, one each to Prisca and Johnny.

"I haven't seen any children at Bugy-Baga's place. But I've noticed a lot of little frogs on the bank of the pond," Prisca said.

"The Witch waits for the little frogs to grow up... The most horrible thing is that Bugy-Baga is planning to feed them to his pet lions! He's got three big lions in the cage, he calls them My Fluffy Pussycats. Recently I've heard Bugy-Baga made a deal with the Witch about prices for children, who will be fed to lions." said Tom bitterly and made a fist.

"Can we ever get out of here?" cried little Johnny.

"There is only one way to run going back across the swamp. Tomorrow we will try it!" spoke Tom surely. "But now we have to sleep."

Tom's voice was strict. He made a comfortable place to lie down. The children obeyed and followed him.

From habit Prisca opened her eyes with the first bird's song. Tom was fast sleep. Johnny woke up and waited, guessing who will wake up next?

"I am hungry," he said. He was happy to see Prisca wake up. "Have we got something to eat?"

Prisca took him to one side.

"Shall we pick up some berries for us while Tom is sleeping?" she said.

Johnny agreed and they went to the nearest strawberry meadow. The children were not scared.

"Nothing bad can happen to us now, we've got brave Tom with us! We are safe nearby him," thought Prisca. She felt good and calm as she did when they'd been at home. She made up big cup out of a dock leaf and it was soon full of berries.

"Johnny, we have to go back now. Catch me!" said Prisca happily and turned around. Suddenly she bumped into the something rough and disgusting...

"What small people!" Prisca heard, an angry voice coming from high above. The children threw back their heads.

"Bugy-Baga!" screamed Johnny.

There was an enormous ugly giant in front of them. He had rough grey elephant-like-looking skin and only one red angry eye. Prisca held Johnny's hand tight and stood back pulling him after herself.

"No one can escape from me!" growled the Giant. "Even if someone is hiding, my faithful slaves will catch them soon."

Saying that Bugy-Baga pulled a young tree out of the soil with anger and broke it over his knee. The scared children pressed themselves together and kept moving backwards. Prisca understood that Tom had already been looking for him. Having grabbed Prisca with his three fingers, Bugy-Baga threw her in his vest pocket. Johnny was thrown straight into another one.

The pocket was so big that Prisca had to sit down and hold the rough material in order not to fall. A minute later Prisca discovered a little hole in the giant's pocket. Through that hole she could see Bugy-Baga's huge legs carrying them up the scary hill they had left yesterday.

CHAPTER 7
IN CAPTIVITY

*H*aving reached his place Bugy-Baga took his vest off and shook the children out of his pockets. Prisca fell down uncomfortably, Johnny gave her a helping hand.

"Tie these little people up somewhere!" ordered the giant to Goklag who had appeared nearby.

An ugly creature pushed the children in their backs with a stake and took them to the water pipe sticking out of the ground. The pipe was connected to some iron railings. The Goklag tied the children's legs tight with a rope to the railings and left them alone. The children sat on the ground trying to catch their breath.

The underground building was in full swing. Not far away from Prisca and Johnny, a few men were building the road out of a marble block. All the work has been done by hand. The people's faces were dripping with sweat. Hands and feet were covered with bloody wounds. There was a big fire on the ground with a huge bowl above it. A few women were cooking something in the bowl. Goklags wouldn't leave the people alone for second, they always kept an eye on them. It seemed the children had been forgotten. It helped them to calm down a bit...

"Where is Tom now?" Prisca was thinking. "What is Bugy-Baga going to do to us?"

"Shall we run?" said Johnny.

"Even if we undo these ties we can't get out of this place." said Prisca bitterly looking at the tall wall. Suddenly her eye caught something familiar. It was the stone which was supposed to show them the way to their village. Prisca recognized it. The biggest crack was pointing to the palace.

Two hours later Goklags brought two women to the children. The women approached closer and put on the grass two bowls of soup and two mugs of water. One woman took two pieces of bread from the pocket of her apron.

"You are the girl from the bank of the swamp, aren't you?" she asked and gave them some pieces of bread. Her eyes were full of sorrow and pain. Goklag pushed her with his stick.

"Go, go!" he ordered.

After they went Prisca said:

"We must eat. We have to stay strong!"

"Do you really believe we'll get home one day?" asked Johnny. He was ready to believe every single word his sister said.

"A man must believe in only the best, this is what our parents used to say to us. Remember?" she answered having no faith in what she had just said.

Suddenly the children heard the familiar squeaking sound of the metal door. Prisca looked at the door with fear, her hart was pumping...

"Can Tom be found?" she thought.

She saw Goklags coming down the stairs. A lot of them. They were moving towards the Bugy-Baga palace. When the door was closed behind them Prisca got her breath back.

"They didn't find him!" she said happily and put her hand up. Johnny clapped her hand.

"High Five!!" they laughed.

In the evening a couple of Goklags came to the little prisoners. Having said not one word they untied the children's legs but tied their hands together. Then the Goklags took the children to the unfinished new road. The children were following in silence. They stumbled very often because of the tight ropes. Prisca guessed that they were being taken to the giant monster.

They reached the big beautiful golden gates. Having entered through the gates Prisca and Johnny found themselves in a fantastic walk lined with wonderful trees. Some kind of roaring from above made Prisca put her head up. The goose pimples covered her all over because of what she saw there... There were three lions in a cage just behind the trees. The biggest one was standing on his hind legs roaring with anger towards the children... However the Goklags took Prisca and Johnny further. Finally the little prisoners were brought to the palace. They were pulled up by the steep stairs towards the big door. At that moment Prisca's biggest wish was never to see a scary and angry Bugy-Baga again... But against her will her legs took her to the door which opened slowly. The children were pushed into the beautiful palace.

Beside the luxury huge furniture and high ceiling the children sensed themselves small and insignificant. Straight in front of them Bugy-Baga was sitting in big armchair.

"Don't look at him!" whispered Prisca to Johnny.

"Tell me where is the naughty boy who dared to escape from me?" – Bugy-Baga began to talk. "Then I'll send you back to The Witch! It's the best that I can do for you."

The giant's horrible voice echoed from the walls.

"Not far from the place I found you I picked this up," said Bugy-

Baga and one of the Goklag stretched out a plate with little pieces of rice bread on it.

"You must have seen that boy, if not be ready for the worst!" warned Bugy-Baga.

After a minute of silence the terrible Giant's roaring made the children jump.

"So, have you seen him or not?"

The children shook their heads.

"No, we haven't..." they said both together. Prisca and Johnny turned their eyes away from Bugy-Baga so as not to see the giant's angry face.

"Put them on the roof of my palace, they will never run away from there!" roared the monster and then added with a smile. "Tomorrow I'll treat my fluffy kittens with a delicious dinner for free."

CHAPTER 8
THE RETURN

*P*ushing the children in their backs the Goklags took them to a big platform near the back wall of the palace. The platform looked like a lift. One Goklag having stood on the platform grabbed the children by their shoulders and dragged them up onto it. Another two Goklags turned a huge wheel and the lift moved up to the roof. The children were pushed away off the lift and onto the roof and left alone there.

Prisca looked around. The huge roof was like a big marble ground with two gigantic Bugy-Baga's footprints in the middle. There were beautiful rose flowerbeds on the borders of the roof. Prisca had never seen such a huge amount of wonderful roses before but she wasn't happy to see them now... The children sat down near one of the flowerbeds. Restless silence came with the darkness. There was a ringing in children's ears.

"I am scared..." whispered Johnny.

"Try to sleep!" Prisca was comforting her little brother.

After he had fallen asleep, Prisca burst into tears. She wished she could fly... In half an hour her tired swollen eyes closed and Prisca dropped off into a deep sleep.

"You are a very special girl," suddenly Prisca heard a familiar voice. "You managed to go through the troubles like no one had before! You are strong enough to help yourself and rescue the Giant's slaves. All that is left for you to do is to go home and tell the people in your village what you have seen here."

"But how can we get home from here?" Prisca asked.

"Plait a basket! You have to hurry up, you haven't got much time... wake up... wake up now!"

Prisca jumped up waking from the short sleep.

"What do I have to plait a basket from?" she asked.

But nobody answered her. Only a big bright moon was shinning in the sky.Prisca cried bitterly...

"It was just a dream... a night dream! I can do nothing! she whispered looking at the roses nodding their head with a mild wind. I can't see anything in here but marble."

The roses nodded their heads even more as they understood her sorrow.

"...and roses... roses! Of course, roses! I'll plait a basket of roses! I should have guessed before," shouted Prisca and jumped out of her place.

Soon big pile of red roses was on the floor in front of Prisca. She remembered the way her father used to plait the baskets at home. Suffering from the sharp thorns and moaning with pain Prisca plaited the basket. Sometimes she couldn't help it and screamed quietly because a rose's thorns were hurting her gentle skin badly.

The beautiful pink colours of the dawn appeared above the hill just when Prisca fixed her basket with the ribbons to make it strong. She put sleeping Johnny into the basket very carefully. Then Prisca sat beside her brother waiting for the miracle. She didn't know what would happen next...? But the miracle didn't come... Only a big black cloud covered the dawn light, and it moved toward the palace very quickly.

The lift made a squeaky noise and the two Goklags appeared on the roof. They carried ropes in their hands.

"You will answer for the master's roses!" they roared, when you are in the cage.

Suddenly Prisca saw that the big black cloud above her head crumbled to hundreds and hundreds black birds. They picked up the basket and flew up and away to the sky with Prisca and Johnny.

"We are flying! We are flying!" Johnny woke up and screamed.

Prisca looked down and saw the birds pecking the Goklags on the palace roof.

"I knew you were her," Prisca heard low quiet voice.

"Dear Crow!" cried Prisca.

"I knew you could get home only from the roof of palace," the Crow said.

"Why didn't you tell me that?" Prisca was surprised.

"You would have been scared. The better day the better deed!" came his answer.

Prisca smiled happily at the wise Bird.

"Maybe you know who was talking to me in my dream last night?" she asked.

"Of course I do ! It was the young fairy Ceya. She is not very skilful yet but she is very kind."

Flying above the Witch's place Prisca waved to her faithful friends the moles down there, who helped them to escape. She was so grateful to them!

"We are getting closer to the swamp bank now! We can't land there, but we'll bring you down to the ground in half an hour." said the Crow.

Prisca watched the birds bringing the basket lower to the earth and leaving them one by one. The kind Crow went round and around above of the swamp bank.

"Take care, brave girl! I wish you all the best, both of you! May Hope, Faith and Love be always with you!" he said flying away.

"Thank you, my dearest friend! I'll never forget your kindness!" answered Prisca with tears in her eyes.

The children stood on the ground, they recognized every little tree in the local forest and laughed happily...

"Look, how many beautiful blue flowers there are here," shouted Johnny. "We can make a big bunch for mum."

"O, no Johnny! We shall leave them for the brave people who will go to rescue Bugy-Baga's slave's. They will need them!"

"Yes, yes ! I'll go to rescue them too! I'll rescue the little frogs and Tom, and I'll take you with me, Prisca!"

The happy children laughed again and ran towards their home sweet home which they could see in a very short distance...

The end

www.ingramcontent.com/pod-product-compliance
Lightning Source LLC
Chambersburg PA
CBHW022156260626
47155CB00018B/2266